WALKUPS
Lance Blomgren

conundrum press

We were seeing the future and we knew it for sure. I saw people walking around in it without knowing it, because they were still thinking in the past, in references of the past. But all you had to do was know you were in the future, and that's what put you there. The mystery was gone, but the amazement was just beginning.

- Brian Boigon, *Newsline*

WALKUPS
Copyright © 2000, 2009 Lance Blomgren
Second edition
New format reprint of ISBN 0-9685161-7-3 with new material
Design and photographs: Justin Stephens

Library and Archives Canada Cataloguing in Publication

Blomgren, Lance, 1970-
Walkups / Lance Blomgren. -- 2nd ed.

ISBN 978-1-894994-37-8
I. Title.
PS8553.L566W34 2009   C818'.5409   C2009-900956-0

Dépot Legal, Bibliothèque nationale du Québec
Printed and bound in Canada by Gauvin
Distributed by Litdistco: 1-800-591-6250

conundrum press
Montreal, Quebec
Greenwich, Nova Scotia
www.conundrumpress.com

conundrum press acknowledges the financial assistance of the
Canada Council for the Arts toward our publishing program.

Canada Council   Conseil des Arts
for the Arts   du Canada

Mixed Sources
Product group from well-managed
forests and recycled wood or fiber
www.fsc.org Cert no. SGS-COC-2624
© 1996 Forest Stewardship Council

FSC

WALKUPS

Lance Blomgren

WALKUPS

Lance Blomgren

#4-345 rue Lachapelle

Up the front stairs, over the entrance of the hardware store, and past the bicycles on the second floor landing. In through the front doors, the stained glass, past the mail-boxes and recycling bins, the ashtray and intercom system. Hiss, echo, refrain. Pull open the inner door then move through the portico, thick smell of cleanser. Across the carpeted lobby, tiled floor and into the stairwell where the wall-sized mirror suspends your blur for a full two strides. Quiet past the landlord's suite on the first floor, past the woman who opens her door whenever she hears a noise in the hall, the sound of muffled television. Follow the corridor past the storage closet, the window overlooking the courtyard. *Faster.* The door is at the end of the hall on the right. Brown like all the others, with a spyhole in the middle. You press your eye to the hole before knocking.

Footsteps on the roof send the cat diving under the bed. Who's there? His head snaps from the pillow, sending a wad of gum flying from his mouth onto the blanket. The afternoon had sagged, pulling him down to the soundtrack of wasps drowning in the greasy puddle of the sink. Now, with furry eyes, he can just see down the hallway and into the kitchen: the table, the small pile of dishes on the counter. Pale overcastness and suspended dust, air like Jell-O. In the kitchen a man with overalls holds the fridge door open with his hip, pouring himself a glass of orange juice. Overhead, someone's pounding the roof with a sledgehammer and, still in bed, the recently-roused napper can smell a faint hint of cat shit rising from under the mattress. "We're here for the renovations," shouts the man from the kitchen. He makes a gesture of salutation with his glass. "Anything we can help you with just ask." "Can you please get the hell out of my apartment?" asks the man in bed. "Talk to the landlord. I just work here."

Apt. d'Amours

The ceiling in the office is damp although it never rains. And I'm on the top floor. The weather is cold, but less cold than I would have thought. The building is clean and quiet, as promised. The kitchen is small and cramped, but the dining room opens onto a large front room, providing a panoramic view of the intersection. The bedroom's cozy, enough space for a small bed. But that dripping water, refrigerator noise, roomtone. I can't get around to unpacking. The mailbox remains empty.

She's certain she set her alarm. Her baby's diapers are so full of oopsie that she wonders how long she has slept. The eyes of the puppies have opened and the three little monsters are wagging their tails with delight under the weight of their mother's sagging teats. The room is not as white as it had been painted, and the mailbox is overflowing with newspaper flyers. Across the street, the old cathedral has been entirely demolished, leaving only a vacant, muddy lot where a long line of well-dressed people shift uneasily in the rain, waiting to pile into their tour bus. She notices something moving across the room, a black line winding its way along the kitchen wall, over the counter and into the next room. A trail of black insects leads from the small hole in the back screen door, down the hall through the apartment, and out the narrow gap under the front door. In the cupboard, her can of Raid is completely empty. She winds the grandfather clock in the hallway. The phone stops ringing long enough to hear the toaster pop in the other room.

5574 *boulevard St. Laurent*

A bottle of wine lying naked on the table. Bread crumbs and an ashtray full of bonbon wrappers. Upstairs someone is playing a trumpet. The others point and laugh at the first person that gets up to leave, pulling on her jacket. "One cheek short of an ass," they chant. "You're one cheek short of an ass."

Apt. d'Amours

An apartment for professionals. Month to month lease: rent paid the first of the month. No exceptions. Garbage day is Tuesday, recycling on Friday. No loud music or barbecues. Small parties and get-togethers are allowed with previous permission by management. No laundry after ten at night. All pets must be spayed, neutered and house-trained. The balconies are not to be used for storage of any kind and no laundry-lines are permitted. Management will water the plants in the hallway and keep the front walkway free of snow in the winter. It is the tenant's responsibility to keep the back staircases clear. Management will not be held responsible for any accidents or deaths that occur on the premises.

78 rue Villeneuve E.

As with many first-floor dwellings, this apartment has no balconies and very little direct sunlight. But it does have a large light-shaft, a vertical tunnel built into the centre of the building itself. One hundred years ago, the city planning office took the problem of light-deprivation into consideration and instigated the mandatory construction of these shafts so every room in a building would receive at least a little light, if not a view. Here, the bedroom, bathroom and kitchen all face out onto the light-shaft: a large octagonal tunnel, almost a courtyard. A ten-foot jump to the bottom. There are tufts of grass poking through the concrete and a mesh wire barrier over the top to keep pigeons out. The last tenant was evicted for lighting a barbecue in the tunnel. The light is grey; throughout the day, this greyness gives these rooms the feeling of being stuck permanently in the late afternoon. Sometimes in the middle of winter, the residents wish they had a little more light, a balcony perhaps, or a suite on one of the higher floors. The days are short and the apartment never seems to have a daytime at all. Sometimes they get restless, pace the length of the apartment. Sometimes they open the kitchen door to let in more light, stand shivering as they look out into the light-shaft.

It's not for everyone, mind you. It's unusual and Mediterranean. But it honestly takes no time at all to prepare. Basically any combination of grains and root-like vegetables will start you off. Cracked wheat, bulgur, rice of all sorts. Leeks, even garlic. As you can see, this time I'm using couscous and Spanish onions.

Steep the couscous in an equal amount of boiling water and let simmer until the moisture's all absorbed. Just like rice. Should be fluffy and light, never mushy. One cup yields about four portions. Can you pass me one of those wooden spoons? When it has stopped steaming, add a handful of black currants, a finely chopped onion, Italian parsley, half a cup of imported Niçoise black olives, a small tablespoon of good quality olive oil, and sprinkle salt to taste. I also used a plump clove of garlic. Don't forget the freshly ground black pepper.

As the couscous cools, place six juicy, sliced oranges in another bowl. Sweetness is the necessity here. You want to cut the oranges into large, crosswise pieces so they soak in their own juices. Release the flavour. See all that liquid? How about passing the red wine vinegar? A splatter does the trick. A funny expression since there's no trickwork about it. And now the oregano. Stir lightly. It's best if you can chill the bowl in the fridge for a few minutes. Everything must be cool and fresh. Excuse me. Why don't you go set the table? This is a small kitchen and all I need to do is scoop the oranges onto the couscous. Just take a seat. Dinner's almost ready and the salad can't just sit around. Once the oranges begin tasting like onions, the charm of the whole thing is lost.

6296 rue Casgrain

The setting sun reflects off the landlord-grey brick apartment. You climb three flights of stairs past a steel barrel of aluminum cyanide and the remaining feathers of a dried-out pigeon. This is where your love of a good joke has gotten you: you live here now. You laugh/cough into your hand as you pass the next-door neighbour on the upstairs landing. He's suntanning in an overly baggy pair of shorts. "Hey, have you seen my cat?" You make a facial gesture meant to imply gentle concern as you speak. "He's been missing a couple of days." The word from the rental agency is that the neighbour hasn't adapted too well socially but is really quite pleasant, which is a polite way of letting you know his eviction notice is in the mail and he should be altogether avoided. Saying what is meant is becoming less and less possible in this environment. He dries his forehead with the T-shirt you'd hung on the clothesline the night before and you decide to drop this line of conversation. You are suddenly at a loss to accurately comprehend the image of his scrotum joined wetly to his thigh ("a leather Hacky Sack soaked in engine grease" you'll write later) and would rather not dwell on it. Besides, he's telling you, "What the doctors call shock is really just the physical, bodily realization that the worst possible scenario isn't quite as bad as originally thought," and you take this as a good time to leave. "I'll let you know if I see your cat," he assures, as you unlock your apartment and step inside. Standing there, you can suddenly feel the inner workings of your abdomen. You might say your heart is racing, but you know it's just your stomach, slumped over, lying absolutely still.

There's a sense of restlessness that comes at night, fog's so dense it dampens my senses like an anesthetist: one to a hundred in reverse, bourbon, cognac, a thick alcohol sleep that turns in my head, turns in my head like a car refusing to start on an autumn night. Fernando once said, "In broad daylight, even the sounds shine." In fog they surface as if trapped in a barrel, as if the head's wrapped in foam. I'm out of Diet Coke and ear swabs. I sit down, then stand up. The clock says 9:32.

#802-10 rue Ontario O.

Upon entering an apartment for the first time, the visitor allows his mind to walk through the rooms ahead of him, scan the layout. He wonders what the view from the balcony will provide, what the kitchen is like, the division of space. He guesses what books he'll find on the shelves, the style of furniture, the artwork and decorations. Every apartment is a variety of vital anatomic constituents (organs) arranged in different configurations along a recognizable axis (skeleton) which, like dogs, allow for a great range of differences within the same basic classification. "Can a Doberman have sex with a beagle?" "Only if they get along." The first-time visitor ponders the possible discerning features this new place might possess, goes searching for the differences which give the space its definition. The first-time visitor reads the rooms for clues.

This is not the case here. *Studio Living*, says the billboard. Here the apartment searches for you. Long before you arrive, this wide-open space has been anticipating your visit. At any time you can dress formally, pick fights, eat oysters with boxing gloves, seduce, take a nap under the table, be a Roman. You look for the signs that would normally reveal the story of a space, give it contrast or depth, but find nothing. You move around the space, step across the buckling floorboards, gaze at the busy street from the massive windows, inspect the utility closets, cupboards, cutlery and houseplants, snoop under the sink, check out the photos and decorations. The apartment eludes you. Instead, it comes at you from all sides, searches out your fears and desires. There's a rickety chair on which you'd be nervous to sit. A long, curved asian eggplant. There's a vomitorium in the back where you'd be able to purge, keep

11

the feast going, or simply unload the visceral sourness of your day. Or you could take a pleasant nap on one of the dozen or so beds littered throughout the room. Here, the space reads you, adjusts itself moment by moment.

Apt. d'Amours

Woke up late to the sound of my own breathing. In the trailing moments of my dream I lifted the toilet lid to discover a cockroach log-rolling for its life on a stray turd. I kept trying to flush them down, but the water pressure was so low they kept floating back to the surface. Through the window I could see a Hydro-Québec worker climbing an electrical pole to fiddle with the wires. In certain positions, as he was working, the man's shadow fell across my bed. At these moments I could see his face, see that he was whistling.

The biology graduate student upstairs had pulled the living room curtains so the daylight wouldn't interfere with the fact that her power had been disconnected. Earlier I had found her note under my door: *Blackout Brunch—Dress Warm, Jane, #308.* But when I arrived there was no food and certainly no other guests. Thick warm air. Running along one wall of her living room was a massive grey metal table that looked like it might have come from an automobile assembly line. The surface was covered with textbooks, flasks and beakers, and dozens of jars filled with beautiful biological specimens. She showed me one of her favourites: a thin yellowish leaf with a remarkable likeness to an adult human hand. As I leaned over the table, I noticed her skin smelled like rubber bands. "So a horse walks into a bar…" she said. Later, she asked me if I had any candles I could spare until the bank cleared the cheque from her research grant. When I returned with the candles, her door was closed and I could hear her moving around inside. I knocked a few times, waited, then left the candles outside her door. On the way back downstairs, for no particular reason, I suddenly thought of Charlie Gardner in Victoria, lying naked in his bathtub, a little pink facecloth barely covering his privates.

5170 rue Durocher

In this photograph, the two brothers are sitting on the sofa squinting. Wrapping paper everywhere. If this were a film their lips would be moving and they'd be talking at the same time. They'd be up to their necks in gift wrap. Already the face of the youngest is the face of someone with something to hide. There are small wrinkles around his eyes that he's proud of. This photo records the moment when the idea struck him, *If only there was a dictionary that would tell me how to act*. He's holding his breath. The walls seem to be squeezing in around him.

#2-383 rue Edouard-Charles

Seventy-three steps from one end to the other. What is called a "shotgun apartment" in New Orleans or "typical immigrant housing" by the city planning office. Indeed, one bullet, traveling straight down the long hallway, is really all it would take. He wanders from room to room, allowing his footsteps to add up. Are you taking your medication? Have you forgotten your keys? He stands absolutely still behind the front door as someone rings the buzzer six times before finally giving up. The cat is purring at his feet. On a nail in the back closet, the last tenant left a yellow baseball cap and there are long-distance calls to Rotterdam on the phone bill. Jetlag. Resting against the wall in the bedroom, his thick blue winter coat has taken on the shape of someone asleep in an airplane seat, huddled uncomfortably against the window. The kitchen spins on its axis. From his position on the hallway floor there's no way he can see the TV, but he can hear it. Captain Picard is asking for all power to the deflector shields. The Enterprise is about to enter a wormhole.

#5-1609 rue St. Hubert

The concierge's footsteps can be heard in the stairwell. On TV the woman sipping coffee is beginning to take on a certain three-dimensional tangibility. In the hallway, someone's unlocking a door, while next door someone else barks with irritation into a telephone. The woman's sipping from a large white cup and flips through the magazine open on the table in front of her—enjoying a nice quiet moment. Yesterday the window wouldn't open; today the TV won't turn off. It's only eight o'clock in the evening. The ice cream's melting down the stick. Somehow a junebug the size of a kiwi has gotten through the window screen and every few minutes the smoke detector beeps a warning about low batteries. Water rushes in the pipes. The concierge's footsteps echo in the stairwell long after he's gone. The woman on TV smiles into the room: "A vacation in every sip." She puts down her coffee cup, keeps reading.

Apt. d'Amours

Comfortable with its own uncluttered dreariness, this sort of apartment building marks a return to the discourse of architectural modesty. Stylishly bleak, but not imposing, these apartments represent a moving back to the city—a neo-urbanity—to celebrate in all its dubious offerings. The doctors downstairs, as well as Mr. Green, the financial advisor on the fourth floor, and even the retired politician and his wife, are all part of this movement. As Mr. Green told me in the stairwell: "To participate in the joy of alienation and misunderstanding that only the city can provide. I suppose all of us here at the Apt. d'Amours must share an understanding of this to some degree." Originally constructed as a mid-sized, humble apartment complex for people of modest means, this building (and many others like it) has been completely overhauled and now provides a semi-fashionable refuge for financially comfortable people seeking an alternative to condominium city living.

The neighbours I've met all seem welcoming and polite. But I still haven't talked to the woman upstairs with the salon-straightened hair or the guy with the two kids downstairs. There's also the guy down the hall who wears a suit jacket and is always carrying his bike. He's about my age and judging from his style of dress seems to come from a similar background or maybe even work in a similar field. He's likely a journalist, maybe a philosophy student—he probably teaches ESL. We have the same sneakers. It is likely we drink at the same bars. I hoped that by moving to this neighbourhood, even this building, I'd be able to avoid his type. Which I guess is to say my type. I've seen him coming or going twice now, but we haven't acknowledged each other even though I held the door for him that day he was wheeling his bike inside.

"Now that I have grown old, I have the feeling when walking through a cemetery, that I am apartment hunting," writes Edouard Herriot. And vice versa.

So "joy of alienation" it is. You can try to change your life... leave your job, seek out new friends, change neighbourhoods, stumble through a new language, take up residence in a slightly expensive example of what is essentially a spruced-up version of a grey socialist housing project and still never really progress beyond what you already are or have been. Perpetually apart from things, perpetually conjoined. It's a kind of happiness.

The children pluck the ants from the cupboard under the sink. The system is established. First into the waiting room of a small yogurt container of water, then one by one dipped into the cooling wax of a large candle with a pair of tweezers. Back in the water of a second container, the wax solidifies around the bodies of the insects, forming a stiff white cast. Next they are set to dry on a clean rag, lined up for inspection. The examiner is the girl with the magnifying glass. Touching the end of a red-hot paperclip to the wax blobs, she lifts them from the line-up and inspects the convulsing creature with the lens. "Your chances of recovery are quite promising," she whispers to some. "I've got some bad news," to others. What a job this is! The medics lay the wounded in bottle caps while the bodies of the deceased are piled onto wedges of toilet paper. Over at the funeral home the ants are laid to rest in matchbox coffins, given last rites. Some children weep from the pews. The director of the funeral home gives his brief condolences from a sofa cushion in the corner. The musicians play the Funeral March on instruments too tiny to hear.

Blueprints of the building spread out in front of you. One is a top view, with each floor inset into the drawing. Your fingers follow the blue lines of the plan, feel the texture of the ink. The paper is old and dry, and shows the building as it was before you were born. You run your fingers over the walls and staircases, storage closets and support beams, follow the contours of the building that your grandfather lived in when he first moved to this city. Each view of the blueprint provides you with a different perspective of his life. Here's the step where he broke his leg, the corner where he stacked his *National Geographics*, the hallway that became a tunnel as he buried himself inside with his collections. Cereal boxes and ceramic tiles. In this blueprint you can see him sitting in his chair, hear his dry lungs. With your fingers, you retrace his footsteps through the apartment.

This Way Out. Condemned. High Voltage. Trucks Only. Telephone. Wet Paint. Don't Cross Police Line. Flammable. Closed for Renovations. Authorized Personnel Only. No Parking. Off Limits. Quiet. Emergency Exit. New Management. Watch Your Step. Hardhat Zone. No Smoking. No Trespassing. For Sale. Information. Danger. Do Not Enter. Stand Back. Private Property. Out of Order. Back in Five. Do Not Disturb. Pay Here.

Apt. d'Amours

The swell of morning traffic. Five thousand kilometres from here, in a room like this one, we used to doze until noon listening to the radio. The paint was blue, the paint was yellow, the paint was abalone satin from the past. I suck my sheets thinking of you. I think: Don't do that. I climb out of bed, I think: Don't do that. Make myself a sandwich: Don't do that. Living alone plays tricks on your mind. "If not this place, then another." Don't stop. Every morning I wake up one minute before the alarm goes off. All of this is too well planned to be a disaster.

Sous-sol. The motion detector in the alley trips the spot-light with any passing mouse, casting the bedroom in yellow through the filter of the curtain. This means it's no longer dusk. But there's never any mice, never any cats—she lets the curtain drop. "I can tell I'm being watched. I know he's out there." She traverses a large pile of laundry with one long stride, then hops onto the bed from three feet out to avoid the surrounding mess: the towels and books, underwear and shirts. She lowers her weight onto the long reclining lump under the sheet, feels it stir. "How does he know where you live?" he asks from beneath the cover.

"I'll never suntan again," he pronounces. The only word that comes to mind is "alabaster," her arms exiting luminous from that robe, stirring pasta. He flips through a magazine as he sits at the table. Apparently, Franz Kafka made the publisher of *The Metamorphosis* promise to never print an illustration of Gregor Samsa on the book-sleeve. Kafka believed an actual image of the insect would belittle the imaginative power of the reader. The kitchen window is at ground-level, and as the man reads he imagines that, from the outside, his head would appear to be sticking up from the ground. But now the window's fogged over. Now the curtains are drawn. He closes the magazine and stands up, moves in next to her. To catch any of the action, you'd have to be inside.

The onions, the garlic, the slices of lemon. The beef still steaming on the plate. Winter was setting in and the dinner guest felt as if he was eating to bundle himself up from the inside. "Imagine actually ingesting a sweater?" he speculates aloud, and the others at the table make faces, look at each other and laugh. They clink wineglasses. He notices his eyebrows are getting damp, that he's breaking out in a sweat. "I swear this food's reconstructing itself in my stomach." More laughter.

Apt. d'Amours

Later in bed and I hereby make the resolution not to eat like that again. I resolve not to get up until winter is over. Polar bears can nap for more than a month on the sustenance provided by a single elk. You can see the distinct shape of a large rodent gradually shrink to nothing as it passes through the body of a sleeping snake. Rabbit ears. Finger puppets. Fish-hooks baited with chunks of egg, Campbell River, and Michael's story about swallowing a piece of bacon tied to a string then pulling it up, pulling and it comes (I hear it, meatwater m eat wat erme a twater me atwater me at) out of a bag. Goddamn it. Beside the toilet now. The two doctors who live downstairs are evidently fixing late-night BLTs, the smell of it coming through the floorboards, making my stomach swim. All employees should wash their hands after eating, no matter what profession. You are what you eat, after all. Not to mention where you've been. I can smell the inside of my nostrils. I pull and pull, but the sweater won't come off.

She returns tired from the Y. She had her own swimming lane for a change. Her face is still hot and she's sweating. In the hallway the door of #8 is open and as she passes she can see that the suite is filled with TVs, covered over in sheets. The tenant appears in the doorway. He is wearing a stupid hat and hasn't shaved in days. "Where were you?" he asks. "Swimming." She can smell the chlorine lifting from herself as she speaks. She smiles and tries to pass, but his face gets in the way. "Why are you wearing that?" He looks like he is choking on himself; he has something to say, but can't get it out. She passes by, shuffling quickly down to her suite, leaving him in the door frame—safe in an earthquake. He's still standing there as she opens the door.

Eventually his usual visitors stopped coming by. The only book in the apartment was a boring one—almost impossible to get past the first dozen or so pages. Although he had ample time to allow himself to catch its flow, and although he continued to persevere, each attempt at reading the book inevitably involved flipping backwards through the pages to remember how he had arrived at the page he had last read. And each time he would end up at the beginning, at the first page with its enticing opening:

> *It is not upwards or down to where I set my gaze, but into, where the mystery of absolute space and immobility is rejoiced. The book told me that as everything moved— nuclei, earth, solar system, galaxies and black holes—one point stood still: a single hinge or pivot on which all matter could move. I am that point. I am the fulcrum. I witness the movement of the all, but remain the promise, the book in the expanse that is the opposite of body, that is blind, mute and deaf, that is not form or mass, not gas, liquid or solid, that is not emotion, intelligence, fact, opinion, order or quality. I am neither midnight nor noon, alive nor dead, error nor truth, but all of them.*

Soon he was avoiding the few phone calls he received. And soon he no longer pretended to himself that he had any interest in the book beyond those opening lines. For ease of reading, he copied the fragment onto a sheet of paper, and then onto another, and then in larger letters onto a larger sheet of paper, and then more. On a whim he wrapped his health insurance card in one of the copies, put it in an envelope, and even ventured outside to mail it to his sister. Back inside the apartment, everything was quiet and warm. He took long naps. After a while, his hunger simply went away, and some days later his thirst. He realized with some satisfaction that he no longer possessed the human constraint of need. He knew that while there was something definitely wrong with him, and that he was clearly getting worse, he nonetheless felt quite good, excited—one might say optimistic.

5433 rue Waverly

Two men stand in a small office, whispering. "I remember when I got my first job," says one to the other. "I was completely shocked to discover there were no beds or sleeping rooms provided for employees on the premises. I thought, where the hell do you nap during your lunch break?" The other man nods his head, scratches at his jowls. A few minutes pass. "Did I ever tell you about the plans for my dream home?" the first man continues. "I want every room to be carpeted with wall-to-wall mattress. That would be so amazing."

Beside my glasses a hill of pocket change, a sculpture of polypropylene, some postage stamps. Windex boot sock hair oil skin brown off white, fragments of insignificance. Already each moment is decelerating, losing its speed, and everything seems predictable and expected. Already I am stumbling down the furniture, nursing my paper cuts in the month of November remembering Mr. Webster's talking bathroom, smoke stained walls....

I ran into Jane in the hallway after my nap. Meeting her made me nervous although I had been secretly hoping to see her all day. I think she sensed this as she suddenly leaned over, blocking my way and whispered, "I have two words for you." She counted them off on her fingers. "Anal. Snake." I was unable to imagine a response, stood there looking dumb. "Definitely not for the faint of heart." And then she told me about her neighbour, Mr. Menard. A few days ago, she bumped into the film editor in the hall. She was on her way out—locking her door—when something caught her attention. Mr. Menard was at the end of the hall, stepping slowly backwards as he watched her, obviously not wanting to be seen. Realizing he'd been caught, Menard tensed up, shrugged, and began walking towards her. His face was bright red and he was carrying a box: Levitt's Roto-Rooter Plumbing Snake. Jane's convinced that he uses this as a bizarre sexual implement. She began making hand gestures, turning the snake in her hand, making wet, sucking sounds until I covered my ears. "Couldn't he just have a clogged toilet?" I suggested. "One doesn't necessarily exclude the other," she said. "And besides, you need to be aware of these things. It should motivate you to dig deeper into the happenings around you. Imagine the things that go on when doors are closed."

7856 rue d'Iberville

A comfortable blanket of second-hand smoke and a layer
of burnt toast. The kind of smell you associate with your
grandma's guest bed and her Lysol sprays. Electric heaters
creaking away. You suppose it's within the realm of possi-
bility that this carpet was once red. Ten years ago there was
a fireplace along this wall, the man tells you, but eventually
the soot became so thick the chimney simply closed up.
Bad lungs, indeed. The man discharges a yellow laugh into
his handkerchief and leads you down the hallway and into
the bathroom. "The damnedest thing." He flicks on the
light. He gives you the hush signal: two knuckles pressed
against his lips, squishing out the colour. Whitenoise like
a gas leak or looped exhaling. "Can you hear it?" It's hard
to tell at first... sssssssssss. The toilet's gurgling and, even
when he's holding his breath in silence, the man's got a
nose-whistle. You cup your ear. Then, beneath the hiss, a
low hum emerges, a cat purring perhaps, then something
sharp like teeth cracking into an apple, leaves rustling, then
the distinct sound of a car struggling to start, the tapping
of a pencil. And then, beneath that, some syllables, wet
lips, sounds becoming words: sssssssstopsssssssssmmmok-
innnngggsssssss. You find your head nodding. "I told you, I
told you." Beside you the man is shaking, his smile pushing
tears out of his eyes. You try to follow the voice but lose it
in the ambient rush of the man's wheeze. "Does this mean
I have to give up my Gauloises?"

Squatting with each leg on a side of the bathtub, she rubs
her crotch up and down the length of his face in long slow
strokes as he sits submerged in the tub. She's still in her
underwear and he can feel the wet heat of her body coming
through the thin fabric, the dogmatic outline of her lips.
The water is getting cold. He can feel his arms go to goose
pimples, his skin pull into itself. The next-door neighbour
is pounding out a fast, ceaseless rhythm on the wall and
the bathwater ripples in unison. Is that voice really saying,
"Get a womb?" His mouth presses into the wet cotton,
stretching the material as his tongue traces patterns in the
folds of her pussy, tries to push inside. He finds himself underwater. Her vulva is pressed firmly against his mouth and
under the elastic of her panties his soapy finger is tickling
her ass in an ever-tightening spiral motion. Looking up at
her through the blur of the bathwater he can see her bite
a knuckle in a poor attempt to stifle her screaming laughter, but even underwater their combined cacophony has
completely blocked out the sound of the angry neighbour.
They'll probably have to move again, of course. They've
been warned. His tongue gets around the elastic of her
underwear and suddenly everything's blue. Tabula Rasa.
Already he can see the angry face of the landlord, the eviction notice taped to his door.

Went by Baby Larry's apartment today to reclaim the yellow arborite table he bought, but never paid me for. He wasn't home so his roommate let me in. She was a little upset as I began to clear off the table, but offered no resistance. The apartment is a split-level cave; the doorways are so narrow I had to dismantle the legs to pull it into the hallway, edge it down the stairs. The words "the devil's day off" come to my mind, then the thought of a TV show made entirely from footage of non-incriminating hidden baby-sitter cams. Shots of the happily bored. It's good to have a dinner table again. Jane's coming over for dinner on Tuesday. There are large gaps around the window frame, a constant draught. Must remember to put plastic over the windows before the weather drops.

The suit-jacket-and-bike-guy is Dustin. I was close in my hypothesis—he does some freelance video editing and teaches English at the brewery in Dorval. He ignored me as I was lugging the furniture in from the car, but knocked on my door as soon as I was done. He was cleaning out his place. Did I want some old music magazines? I wasn't sure. He's from Massachusetts. Been in town a few years. He's seen Höfer's latest film, and is also about halfway through the Ovalle novel. He told me a story of the elderly man who used to live in my apartment, and how the old guy once asked him to help look for his dentures. I took the magazines and he asked me where I had bought my jacket—he had one like it, he said. Then he asked if I could take in his mail. He was going out of town and would leave me a key, it would be a great favour, etc. I wanted to make

39

an excuse, but couldn't come up with anything. As soon as I agreed to the task, he was in a hurry. He thanked me brusquely and informed me he'd push the mail key under my door later in the afternoon.

"Hamlet hoped/ the pill would stimulate/ activity/ rather than/ acting." He places his words right in your path, reading them the way some people drink milkshakes. "Severely rejected testicles/ hurling a huge waterfall/ of the eye." Delaying the final sip. You trip over them, bruise yourself on their window sills, or slip into them like wet pajamas, find yourself drifting in butter. "Listen to this," he says, nudging your arm with his elbow. He clears his throat. "Stupid as he is/ He asked the same question/ As you."

You squeeze past into the next room. In his highchair the baby is staring intently at an old dictionary. It is one foot thick and contains the kind of illustrations that are now reserved for bible pamphlets and educational comics. As Bobby became older, he began to notice there were certain dissimilarities between his father's body and his own. While his father's chest was covered with a thick coat of brown hair, Bobby's own chest remained pink, smooth and hairless. The dictionary smells musty and alive, and each page carries the scent of everyone who has opened it, and the baby is entranced by their stories. Right now Dar is doing the dance of the six sailors, and his friend Sara is using the book to see over the heads of the onlookers. "Action Adagio," declares the man, relishing each word as he enters the room. "Asserting that/ 'He hit the ball'/ Is vigorous activity."

5746 rue Clark

You in your shorts make clear the tragedy of our loss of fur.
Artificial respiration. Knees taking all that breeze.

The gist of her husband's thesis is, "Architecture is war." He spends hours in there each night working on his dissertation and often doesn't come to bed at all. Where he was born, she knows, he gained first-hand knowledge of the ways in which construction and urban design gave form to violence. He has spoken so often about the experience of growing up in that place of new streets, commerce centres, condominiums—the sudden acts of erasure and the shocking implementation of order, social and structural order, that would follow soon after—that these days he hardly speaks at all. Only those periodic exclamations of anger or delight from behind the closed door. He rarely emerges to take supper with the family.

Her own thesis is on the social history of coprophagia, so she knows that within the span of history her husband's story is not unique. She knows that like many others he has seen unspeakable things. She knows that he has become lost in the things he can't bear to look at, and understands that he finds comfort and even wisdom there; she has spent years studying how we find food in the most literal and metaphorical of shits. She can help him. She remains sympathetic toward his upbringing, supports his erratic process and strange drives. She even agrees with him that the story of order, as told by either the city planners or the generals, is a story of erasure itself. She loves him.

But this is too much. Torqued buildings and ragged interiors, the influence of temperature on steel, the open-floor concept of ruin and structural collapse. The dignity of the

43

explosion. She can't have that, not on top of the muffled laughing, the late night ordering of pizza. The disappearance of the paper towel and emergency batteries. The Ravel on maximum volume. The dwindling bank account and the unclean boy from school who is hanging out with her son, his silver rings. The smoke from under the door. "This is no longer architecture criticism," she appeals from the hallway, anger growing. "This is no longer sociology." *When we sleep, we should just sleep. When we shit, we should just shit.* Long before somebody calls the police, she has kicked a hole in the door.

Apt. d'Amours

Whose stories are these? "Crazy bait"? Reminds me of Steve, holding out his hand so Monkey could sniff the bandaged wound and him saying, "My thumb is fucked up like an old piece of fried chicken." My friends' stories and secrets become verbal ready-mades. Their experiences become my own.

It's raining outside, can't concentrate. I like the way Jane somehow manages to enter a room two seconds behind her smell. Nice effect. The improbable gravity of her haircut. The full-spectrum light bulbs aren't working at all, nor the Vitamin D. My skin is getting pasty and my thighs are breaking out in violent acne—all brought on by the changing weather. Early signs of mental chafing. A sad and funny story. A large silver exhaust pipe snakes from my gas furnace through the apartment. I stand beside it to keep warm. Put my hands in my armpits. I think of heat waves.

6296 rue St. Dominique

The rooms are wide open and chilly, but it never seems cold.
There is nothing to be said, so the two of them say nothing.
The balcony is growing a layer of snow and all sound is
slowly being sucked out of the air. This could be Stalingrad,
1944, but it's not. There's a smell of beer and bread. No cab-
bage. On the couch they doze into each other like pillows.

She carries the plastic container with her everywhere, to bed, to the bathroom. During the day she carries it in her purse, takes it to work. Back at home it is on the nightstand, under her bed, on the shelf in the hallway next to the keys. The container used to hold something dense and moist, likely made from milk solids, but not any more.

His attempts to apologize, reconcile, improve the mood went unacknowledged and soon he realized a more subtle approach would be needed. He plans a surprise attack of inaction. The container never leaves her sight; numerous times a day she peels back the lid and looks inside with an expression of curiosity that resembles discomfort. After some time the contents begin to change colour.

He sleeps sitting in the armchair by the front door, and during the day he sits there awake. She is liable to walk by at any moment, with her luggage in tow. He resists the inclination to step into the bedroom, open the buttons on her pajama top, and rest his head on her stomach.

When he wakes, the container is on the end table next to the armchair. The sudden recoiling of his limbs upsets the container, sends it rolling across the carpet where it falls open, releasing its insides. The note on the fridge says, *Desire is the most unaccommodating of emotions*, but he doesn't notice it until the next day. The small growth on the side of his neck feels tender. It takes a mirror and some deep picking with the tweezers to get it out.

868 rue Champagneur

They are in the kitchen, sitting at the table just a few feet from each other, passing the cat back and forth while the other pecks at the keys on the laptop. "Your turn," one says. The other types the words *random pork* into the search field and up pops the library of images, including the one of the two guys in pig costumes apparently in some sort of altercation. The next passing of the cat and keyboard results in a picture of a hillbilly with his collection of dust. The cat has given up struggling a while ago: the silicone enhanced buttocks slathered in marmalade, the dried out pickles on concrete steps, the time-line of moustache styles throughout history. They suffer from creative temperaments, but often take work in offices. They look for inspiration. There is no way they can make this up.

Apt. d'Amours

Something catches my eye. A question mark crouching in the corner of the room. Something barely visible, insignificant, something I could probably ignore or stamp out of existence. Smaller than my shoe. I shouldn't think about it, pay it any attention—to acknowledge it is to bring it to life. It's too late. Suddenly there's another question mark, peering up from under the orange armchair, then another. In the living room, the questions grow, spin, and divide. Surround my feet. They fill the space up like water, spill into the kitchen and run down the hall. Soon I'm drowning in questions. This is the way with question marks. At some point you breathe them in.

8561 rue René-Labelle

You are fearless. You have the know-how to turn your apprehension into virtue. Not too long ago you would have been queasy and nervous in this situation. You had trouble accepting things for what they really were. You would drain the battery trying to start the empty car, so to speak. Sheer repetition has made you natural. Your moves are fluid and confident. You are looking forward for it to begin. You look terrific and feel great. Here goes.

The first room is the central resting space. Admission to this room is a dirty or sad story. You take off your shoes and place them in line neatly along the west wall, beneath the long row of windows. You sit in an uncomfortable chair covered with a sheet and wait. Meals are served. When your body's feeling good you put on the pair of shoes at the front of the line.

When you enter the room the first thing you notice is the floor. It's soft underfoot and shimmers as you walk over it. The next thing you notice is the topless man. He is hunched over a table, holding his forehead in his hand, and is eating mechanically from a ceramic bowl. Behind him, a woman systematically pulls out the hairs from his shoulders with a pair of tweezers. They lift into the air, catching the breeze from the open window before settling on the floor. The air sparkles. Your skin becomes prickly; you cross the room and exit through the other door.

The next room is a no-man's land. It acts as a kind of waiting room or meeting place—a disconcertingly comfortable room where all the furniture is covered in live skin. Everything you touch is slightly warm to the touch. Meals are served. The air is tropical and the music, if anything's playing at all, is always Brazilian. As you sit with the others, the conversation inevitably turns to the weather or a re-cap of the day's events. It is possible to spend days here. There are bottles of moisturizing cream sitting on little plinths. Every few hours you rub some cream into the skin around you to keep it soft and pliable.

You open the closet and are horrified by what you see. You head east, down the hall to the back room.

You enter this room by a series of rounded pink stairs. There's a well-worn path cut into the tiles. Remove any restrictive clothing and place it in the bins provided. Insert ear plugs. As you move into the room you notice the vibrations, hear the noise become louder as you continue walking. You can feel the vibration in your stomach and chest, a low rumbling sound that causes an involuntary contraction of the diaphragm and throat, a sudden fibrillation of the heart. The sound grows inside you. You open your mouth as you pass through the room to let the noise come rushing out.

Unplug your ears. You are now in a room full of birds. It is dark, but you can see movement as the room changes shape around you. You can feel wings brushing your face and legs as you enter. Your eyes become accustomed to the blackness and begin to make out shapes. You take a seat on one of the benches by the east wall and remain still. Birds land on your shoulders and nestle in your hair. When you've had enough, or if you are afraid of the creatures, leave by the sliding glass door.

The bathroom is a short walk towards the back. In the shower there is a planter of fresh herbs and a pair of scissors. There is also a chair. The faucets are decorative so you must stand on the chair to open the skylight, let the rain enter. Cut the herbs into fine pieces and rub them into your skin as you wash. The birds that have followed you into the bathroom fly out through the hole in the ceiling.

Emerge from the bathroom clean and make your way to the next room. The smell of lake-water and moist dirt propel you in the right direction. The room is packed with your closest friends; there is only enough room to stand. There is a stainless-steel machine in one corner and a conveyor belt that dispenses ceramic bowls filled with a sweet-smelling grain. The attitude is convivial and everyone is speaking in animated tones between spoonfuls of roughage. Beverages are served. Time dissolves into a static moment of eating and dancing.

The party moves on. The walls of this room are curved and spongy and every surface you touch seems to respond with a sensual counter-pressure. The air is thick and salty. You lay on the soft floor. Using only your mouth, you try to discover the identity of the others. You run your tongue over the other bodies to locate their position, work your lips over their faces. To leave the room, you run your tongue over the walls, searching for the exit.

The exit is always cast in late-evening light. Somewhere outside there are street-noises, muted voices, seagulls squawking. The surfaces of this room are covered with a layer of lard, and you find it hard to maintain your balance in such a slippery environment. The lard gets on your hands and face, soaks through your clothes. The floor of the room is slanted slightly into the middle, and as you become greasier you begin to slide into the centre of the room. You slip and fall into the thick coating of lard and fight to stand up. The room starts moving; your feet slide around beneath you and you fall again. This time your hand slips through a small hole in the floor. You try to push yourself up, but your other hand goes through. Soon your head is through the opening, and you find yourself hanging there, looking down to the street. You can feel your weight behind you, pushing you through.

The band is playing music designed for sexual pleasure. The drummer is banging out a rhythm in 9/8 time that synchs the vibrating of your eardrum with the brain waves of the sexual response centre in your head. It hits everyone in the groin at the same time. A man playing billiards sends the cue ball off the table, and someone spills her drink. The dancing begins: floorboards flex under the weight of the bass line. Everyone looks so sexy in his or her New Years' outfits that the man at the back of the room can hardly stand it. He needs to photograph this. He pulls his camera out of his bag and sets it on auto timer. 10, 9, 8, 7 .... At the count of two he throws his camera high in the air and manoeuvres to catch it. The shutter snaps just before the camera falls into his hands. To this day you can see the photo on the man's refrigerator. Pairs of legs, skirts, fancy shoes. Not one foot touching the ground.

Feeling jumpy. When I woke up this morning, Jane wasn't in bed. Somehow the condom had stayed on. Surprised how strong the room smelled of sweat and stale air, considering I'd been immersed in it. A flickering image: Jane on her hands and knees, checking out her ass in the wall mirror, grinning: "What's the big deal? I don't get it." But her clothes and jacket weren't draped over the armchair at all, there were no dinner dishes on the table. Think, think. Wasn't there something about crêpes and smoothies? If it wasn't for the lingering scent of formaldehyde it would be possible to believe she hadn't been here at all. No note or message. And in the next room, my computer was humming away, just as I left it.

Apt. d'Amours

An article from the *Gazette*:

> *MONTREAL—In the late hours of the morning, police were called to the residence of M.D.S. Harris, Director of the Phoenix International Life Sciences medical research organization, after an unidentified man broke into Harris' Outremont condominium. According to the police, the man scaled the building's rear security fence, climbed the fire escape, and entered the apartment through the back door without tripping the security alarm. The intruder, claiming to be a former Phoenix test subject, terrorized Harris and his wife for more than three hours until another resident alerted the police to the excessive noise coming from the Harris suite. "They are usually the quietest people," commented Jan Boucher, the Harris' downstairs neighbour. "I knew something was wrong." The assailant escaped just as police were arriving. Rick Treadwell, Harris' spokesperson, said the family was fine, but still in shock from the incident. The authorities are investigating possible motives for this crime.*

Explosion of ice flakes on the afternoon air. An ending on the horizon, or opening credits? You sit up with a start. The window has frosted over and you have to scrape the glass with your fingernails to see out. Footprints on the back balcony, an unseen animal rubbing its back against the bricks for heat. Edges of approaching darkness. Indoors, snow is filling the fireplace and the Presto Log crackles with wetness. Your glasses are fogging over. Just a moment ago your lover's flesh felt like putty beneath your ass as you straddled him on the couch, cold as the ice you were melting over his shoulders. There's water pooled in the small of his back; one deep breath would upset the balance, send the freezing liquid down his sides onto the blanket. External obliques. And across the courtyard, another snow-blindness: poinsettias, wintergreen, discarded Christmas trees. Balconies full of snow. Apartments shut up against the cold, almost abandoned except for the rooms where winter creatures enter, seeking warmth. And your heat too, draining quickly: frozen glances, icy breath, cold shoulder. The blanket far too thin. Conversation on the verge of shattering. *Break it. Don't.*

No one realizes that every time Mayor Bourque becomes sexually excited, a young man in Mile End becomes simultaneously aroused. Bourque is late for a morning meeting and forgets to take a shower; across town the young man's erectile tissue begins to throb for no apparent reason. It happens that a small number of people are born with super-sensory olfactory lobes. "Forget about justifying your work," the man says to his roommate suddenly, shifting positions in his desk chair to accommodate the swelling. The roommate sits on the sofa across from him and unleashes an exaggerated nod. "You just have to trust it." The young man draws bunnies, the second writes stories about anosmiatics—people who have lost their sense of smell. I can smell you being invisible. At his private health club, Mayor Bourque is working up a sweat playing squash; his thoughts turn to the white thighs of his lover. The young man at the desk commences a flurry of sketching: bunnies, bunnies. The roommate thinks he hears the balcony door click open, then he thinks he didn't.

586B rue Peel

With your fingers in your ears you can actually believe you're not on this sofa. You dry your mouth on your hands and your hands on your pants.

"So although they were right in front of you, you couldn't actually see them?"

"That's right. They were standing in a circle around me, but were giving off a light so blinding it seemed that from under my squint there was nothing there at all."

"You're going to be all right."

"I understood what they were saying, but they were talking so loudly I couldn't actually hear them."

"It's been nice talking to you."

I need to get out of here. I can't stand the way they look. The only place I can properly get sick is out-of-doors.

She set fire to her mailbox to destroy the evidence and began hiding the telephone bills and her purse. Her perfume is new luggage smell. Her lips are a blur. You step back into the hallway without inhaling or mentioning the words "chemical spill." And then you're onto something else. From the second-storey window you watch a car's wheels lock up like the voice skidding from your lips. And it hits you. The sun's come up hours ago and now the only music is the sound of ventricles popping as the picnic gets going inside your chest. The relish.

A kid tripping on the edge of the throw rug.

Who were those people with eyebrows pulled over their eyes?
They invited me to their party but forgot to draw me a map.
There's only so many ways you can piece together an evening. I
thought I'd tried them all.

Apt. d'Amours

A semi-wilted spider plant showed up in the hallway at
some point. After a week or two I finally decided to bring
it inside and give it some water. In the afternoon, the repairman from the telephone company finally retuned. The
static interference—almost an echo—had started innocu-
ously enough in the receiver but had quickly taken over
the phone line completely, leaving me at the mercy of the
public booth in the laundromat around the corner. No
word from my parents; I need a job. The repairman's first
inspection had yielded nothing except a $55.00 bill. But a
new phone was no help at all, and neither was a new cable,
so now he was back, tearing the molding from the base of
the utility room wall, cutting into the drywall, crouching
there, and all I could do was concentrate on maintaining a
careful inhalation rate, breathe steadily through my mouth,
pay strict attention to closing off the function of my nostrils
without actually reaching to plug them. Even the memory
of the repairman's previous visit, that almost scentless
odour of revulsion, made the back of my throat itchy. For a
company that employs hundreds I couldn't believe I'd get
the same man twice. How to account for that? I opened the
balcony door, an attempt to steady myself, allow some air to
circulate, but the unease continued to escalate. The repairman was looking at me funny, seemingly unable to breathe
himself. His eyes didn't look right. Without fixing the line,
he was quickly up and moving: "Some other call. We'll get
back to you." My own panic evaporated as if it had never
been there, latched onto something else, and I actually
found myself stepping after him into the hall, apologizing
as he walked away holding his nose. But like the first time,

his presence continued to hang in the air until well into the evening. In the kitchen, the plant on the table by the window was already doing much better; it seemed to have small flowers on it. Tomorrow, a cell phone.

The making of transitory domestic architecture, of public housing and rental units, is a major coalescing gesture in the urban environment, bringing together many flows of social activity into a complex stream. Amidst the current of "events" that best describe the socio-spatial reality of the modern city—the osmosis of culture and commerce, socialization and mediation, the organic and inorganic—balconies face each other, staircases and walls are shared.

How then to account for this hobbit hole? Two rooms, each under 60 square feet in size, with a kitchen in the hallway between them; the bathroom with its own nest of flies teeming in the drop ceiling. Any current theory of housing, any accepted syntax of space, design and function, is largely unhelpful to adequately describe this apartment. Unless you're very thin or very short there would be little opportunity to move around. Any dynamic of family activity or convivial exchange would quickly bottleneck here. This place is an architectural example for a society of bachelors, individualists or monks. This is Yoda's place in the city.

Vernacular architecture, we are told, is situated outside the progressive span of history. It is not disposed to style or fashion. It is too situated in its present-tense temporality to follow the fancy of trend or to imagine its future. There are the mud domes from the upper Volta River, the Dogon cliff dwellings, the carved houses in the rock faces of Provence. There is the troglodyte architecture of Siwa, Eygpt and Shanxi, China. And then there is this apartment. Here, you can believe you are living off the grid, in a tree house or hut. With survival as the only constant underlying our living spaces, one could then say that this apartment remains vernacular, immutable, serving its purpose to perfection. As an example of urban architecture however, this apartment is a folly, an exhibit in the museum of housing.

"How quaint," they say, these visitors. "How primitive, how noble." They marvel at the miniature furniture, at the literal denotation of the word bedroom, the bold anachronism of the 1990s refrigerator-freezer which takes up one third of the kitchen. The oil paintings in the living room are the size of photographs. The TV is a radio. The large creatures of the Late Holocene survey the spectacle through the small front window, their eyes against the glass.

1861 rue St. Grégoire

Empty oil bottles, newspapers, snow shovels and hose. Scent of gasoline and something brown. Relative economies. In the crawlspace under the floorboards the boy is earning a small fortune sifting through the accumulation of rubbish, searching for the boxes of Christmas lights. "Can't see them, Dad." The flashlight is growing weak. Dragging in the dirt behind him, the garbage bag of newspaper and rags powders the air, and the boy is unable to see the cobwebs until they're already stretched across his face. *More scared of you*, more scared of you. There's this new stereo he wants to buy so badly. Beside the back wall there are some paint cans, and beside the paint cans a small clump of fur. Crumpled yellow fur and a few bones. And beside that, the missing boxes. "Runts in every litter," his friend's mother once said, "need to be put out," and he's backing toward the opening in the darkness, grabbing whatever junk he can on the way. "Couldn't find them." The boy emerges dusty from the hole. He hands over the bag, and then it's on to washing windows, stacking boxes, painting the back staircase, to start with. For the rest of the afternoon the boy feels his father's glances as they work, eyes on him like lost change in the dirt.

At 1:00 AM every night the bar downstairs suddenly comes alive, with unyielding bass tones coming through the floor. But it is quieter down the long hallway, back in the room of saplings. The young trees look like twigs in their flower pots but if you look at them long enough, agree to stay with them for a minimum of four hours—longer stays are also encouraged—and embark on a ritual of meditation, observation and reflection, then you can witness their slow assertion from dormant, leafless sticks to something that is exploding in slow motion. So when the bar closes for the night, but the ripples in your cup of coffee remain perceptible, you are not surprised. Nor when the plumbing bursts, sending water onto the pool tables below. In fact, you are not surprised to notice that the reverberations caused by these trees, and your attentiveness to them, soon renders the noise from the bar almost powerless. The guests come and go. Trees, it has been purported, grow in response to noise; they respond to talking, music or even the radio. These trees in this apartment have that and more. There are drawings, stories and toys for these trees; there are the odd words "Guest Ghost Host" like some sort of mantra. And so now they're ripe with foliage, thick with themselves, standing a couple of feet tall. Now they're growing into the floor. The guests leave with scratches on their limbs, lungs enlivened as they burst with oxygen.

Apt. d'Amours

Good morning,

Today I'm in a much better state then when I saw you last. Sorry about not calling last night. Work is very busy. I didn't want to call you so late. Sometimes I feel like quitting and resent the endlessness of it all. But then something fascinating comes up in the research that keeps me going. Some say obsessed... more polite people, like Professor Blake, say driven. And this leads to more late nights and more pressure and I feel like quitting. I hope that makes some sense.

I don't think I'll have the time to meet your parents next week. Next time? I want to see you (I want that massage) but can't handle too many schedules these days. I promised myself I would not get sidetracked until the project is done which is sometimes hard to remember when I'm with you. I'm worn out.

I'm taking next weekend off though. I have a couple housey things to do, but will have some time. Saturday?

With affection,
Jane

8393 rue St. Michel

Calm voices, stern voices, irritated voices, voices hysterical with anger. Then laughing, the sound of voices apologetic and tender. When everything's quiet, the boy turns over in his bed and quietly pulls himself from beneath the cover. He pulls a section of his vertical blind to the side and looks out his bedroom window. On the balcony the two of them are huddled together under an umbrella, sharing a cigarette in the pouring rain.

Apt. d'Amours

Mme. Lafrenière, the recently divorced woman upstairs, knocked on the door, waking me up. She knocked once, a single sharp rap that stood out in my dream like an expected, predetermined moment and I immediately became aware that I was sleeping and willed myself awake, crawling through improbable levels of slumber to find myself back in bed. My ears were still ringing when I opened the door. Her sink was clogged and she wondered if I had a plunger and some Liquid-Plumber, which lucky for her I did. I was just getting back to sleep when Mme. Lafrenière knocked again. She wasn't able to get the drain open, and wondered if it wouldn't be too much trouble for me to come up and help.

Her apartment is immaculate. Recently renovated. Tiled floors, new countertops, massive refrigerator. Scandinavian design—everything white. Shøp. Extremely spacious for a two bedroom. It wasn't the sink drain, but the garbarator. I told her she would need a professional plumber, but she insisted I at least try to unclog it. I emptied the Liquid-Plumber into the hole, ran some hot water and began plunging. At first, there was no pressure, as if nothing was blocking the pipe at all. But after a number of pumps, I could feel the pressure begin to build. I stopped and looked into the pipe. A low wet sucking—the sound of something viscous and sticky—but nothing to see. I pumped hard a few more times then pulled the plunger away. A heavy sulphurous odour poured quickly into the room. I looked into the drain, but still couldn't see anything. Mme. Lafrenière passed me a flashlight. It was then that I noticed it: a frothy white liquid not too far down into the pipe. The smell was

73

overpowering. Suddenly I realized the stuff was coming up into the sink. It was thick and gelatinous, like rotting milk, and Mme. Lafrenière was saying, "I didn't pour anything down," and the stuff was rising in the sink and I simply panicked. I switched on the garbarator and slammed the plunger over the hole until the sticky clog began to recede, slip its way down the pipe. I continued plunging for another five minutes after it disappeared. I think I might have been a little hard on Mme. Lafrenière when I left, although she had been so thankful and apologetic. I'm still going to report her to the manager though. She should be a little more careful with what she puts down the sink.

Late night, listening to CBC 93.5 FM on the floor of her living room. Brave New Waves. An extended solo on two wind machines. The two of them are sprawled on different sides of the room, and he wonders if the sexual tension is entirely his own.

She had tried to swipe the old, silver, hand-sized transistor radio from the knick knack store on Duluth. The salesman caught her when the radio slipped out from under her shirt and landed on the front steps. The sight of the radio had jogged a memory so deep that its very existence—the fact she was even thinking of it now—was proof she would never have thought of this incident again. It had disappeared from her mind and had ceased to exist. But thanks to the radio…. She told the salesman she could suddenly picture herself in her childhood bed, listening to the morning news. Bed. Jennifer from grade three laughed on the bed until she passed out cold: the first and last time she came to visit. The salesman let the radio go for $20 and a promise never to steal again. The antenna was bent from the fall and the silver plastic a little scuffed, but the radio still had good reception.

She steamrolls herself three times across the room until she nudges up beside him. He can't contain his grin. "Now that is a great song!"

6287 rue St. Dominique

At any given moment the silver belly of a 747 could be seen flashing in the sky through a lattice of clotheslines. Across the alley the doghouse in the backyard remained empty, covered in snow. A man in a bathrobe came out the sliding back door, rattling some kibble in a metal bowl. "You can't ignore me forever," he yelled. Steam rose from his slippered feet as he stood there, the snow melting around them. A flock of pigeons landed on a clothesline, and from her vantage point behind the curtain the woman could watch them lose their balance in the wind, fall into flight, then circle back up to resume their watch on the wire. In the frozen afternoon brightness she could see the man's skin redden, the dog food scatter in the snow as his shivering became more pronounced. "Have it your way," he yelled finally, retreating back inside with his bowl, sliding the door shut behind him. Already the pigeons were gray smudges in the snow. Behind the curtain the voyeur straightened up. Deep in her stomach something growled.

He's begun to see things in terms of hours instead of days or years. The alarm on his watch goes off. In 192 hours he will be thirty, or 262,800 hours old. He has to arrive at work in 56 hours; 1104 hours to go before his next vacation. How long has it been since he last saw him? He checks his watch again. Almost 98 hours. He sets his watch alarm ahead one hour.

Mental feedback loop of an insomniac stuck on a single thought. I'm possessed with the sudden desire for all my friends to remain broke or throw away their money. It skips rope in my head. Everyone's writing an autobiography; I can hear the sound of keyboards clicking in different rooms all over the city, the echo of my friends typing steadily in sparsely decorated apartments. There are overflowing bookshelves and furniture hauled in off the street. I'm haunted by an imaginary conversation, a line spoken with eager insistence to an attractive couple at a party. "There's something happening. Madcow. Pigpest. Humania. Self-ingestion. Promise you'll never write about missing children again." The effect is not without an element of dread, these thoughts repeating, nudging me around the edge of sleep. It dangles in front of me and I keep rolling over in bed, looking for that spot. I love these people and think of them often, up late, writing away all over town. Then suddenly I'm terrified they are killers, terrorists involved in some terrible, misleading hoax that's physically insinuating itself into our bodies. My tongue is dry. It tastes like itself, so I know it has been bitten.

Out in the hallway, I could hear her voice. I quietly un-latched my door and slowly peered outside. At the end of the corridor, Jane was leaning against the doorframe of #208 talking to Dustin in low tones. I couldn't hear what they were saying. She put her hand on his arm in a gesture of gentle reassurance and they embraced solemnly for several seconds before straightening up. I leaned back into the doorway to listen. His voice picked up. He had something for her. A book? Her response revealed that she was genuinely excited to receive this present. I took another look. They were leaning into each other again. Back inside the doorway I continued to listen. Their voices were quiet, too low to hear anything with certainty. Jane's words seemed at once empathetic and firm.

4289 rue St. Émile

Overlooking the terrace of an Italian style café from the vista of her second-storey kitchen window. A young girl folds a newspaper flyer into halves. A younger girl wields the scissors, begins snipping. A moment later a chain of hearts emerges. Laundry detergent, chicken breasts, a stray lip, some teeth. The two giggle as the hearts flap in the breeze, the chicken meat and lips waving like some sort of flag. Wagging lips and dancing chicken! Wagging lips and dancing chicken! Soon they're in hysterics and the sale items look like they might come flying off the paper as the wind picks up. Then it happens. On the windowsill there's an alarm clock blinking out the wrong time and a limp aloe plant blocking the view. The voyeur jumps up to see what's going on. By the time she locates the scene, an unhappy looking man is pulling some soggy newsprint out of his bowl of soup—Tide and teeth. The two girls are facing the other way, holding amazingly straight faces.

The roommates get up at 7:30. The woman has the alarm clock; she wakes the man with a gentle knock on his bedroom door as she shuffles down the hall to the bathroom. 7:35. He lies in bed as she brushes her teeth and showers, listens for the spray of water, waits for it to end. She takes long showers—never less than fifteen minutes—then lingers drying off, brushing her hair. She hums to herself. On her way back to her bedroom, she knocks on his door a second time to make sure he's awake. Two raps. The roommate grunts. 7:55. 7:56. While she dresses and blow-dries her hair, the roommate pulls himself up, puts on his robe, stumbles to the bathroom for his shower. He's quick: five minutes. Any longer the water runs out and he gets cold. He doesn't brush his teeth. 8:05. He walks back to his room to dry himself off and get dressed. Three to four minutes. They cross paths for a few minutes in the kitchen. They speak briefly, announce their daily schedules. He will pour himself a glass of milk, and make himself a single piece of toast which he'll let cool on the counter while he puts on his shoes, gets his bag and jacket together. Clockwork: he'll be out the front door with the toast in his hand at 8:13. She eats a big meal—eggs, coffee, toast, sometimes bacon—lingers over her breakfast at the kitchen table reading junk mail or a magazine. She'll sit there a long time hardly moving, reading and drinking coffee in a calm, relaxed state. You have to be patient. Sometimes it seems like she'll never finish. But then it happens. She'll look at the stove clock and realize she's late, snap up from her chair, unleashing a series of profanities and groans. 8:50. 8:52. Agitation sets in. She moves rapidly from room to room, starting one task then moving on to another. She folds laundry with her toothbrush in her mouth. She'll check her day-planner, put cream on her face and ponder the contents of her backpack for an unbearably long moment. Don't let her excited state faze you, her speaking out loud to herself as she searches out her keys. Remain calm. She could change clothes, start cleaning her desk. It's possible she'll make a telephone call to alert someone she's a bit behind schedule. She may even turn on the television to check the weather before she steps out the door. But it'll happen. You should count on a possible wait-time variable of 45 minutes to almost two hours. Bring something to drink. She'll exit the apartment from the back door, walking fast, and descend the fire escape to her bike. Wait until she disappears down the alley before making your move. Sometimes she turns back, realizing she's forgotten something. The back balcony is almost completely obscured by the tree: only passers-by and cars can see you from the alley. Be casual. There's two spare keys in the clothes-pin box by the laundry line. Gold for the bolt, silver for the handle. Remember your gloves. Leave everything as it was. If the roommates don't notice anything different, they won't even realize what they're missing.

#304-3620 avenue Ridgewood (Le Four Thousand)

Not the row house on rue Gounod, where he used to live with his parents, but this modern building where he now with his grandparents. They had left for church and he was alone in the place. He ate some cereal, loaded the dishwasher, and put an armful of newspapers in the recycling bin. He wiped his fingerprints from the reflective surfaces. In the study, he took the coat hangers of laundry off the rails of the treadmill and hung them in the closet. He took off his jeans and T-shirt and looked at himself in mirrors. Then he turned on the treadmill and ran in his underwear at top speed for ten minutes before collapsing on the carpet in front of the sliding balcony door. Catching his breath, he stared at the small hole in the ceiling where, even here, the animal had been letting itself in.

When he told me, I didn't believe him. How do they get the microwave to work while the door's open? "Why, they just jimmy it open with a fork or knife." No way! "It needs to be an older model, but with thirty or forty seconds on defrost you get an instant, delirious fever. Disgraceful." Finally I saw it with my own eyes. The stairs were being repainted and the workmen had moved the large potted plant out of the way. I had to squeeze myself by it to move down the hall. It was there, just before the stairwell, that I passed #104. The door was open and as I moved past, I could see it all, even in the brief moment they fell into my field of vision. It was Jean the teachers' kids, Marie-Claude and Gus. The two of them were standing on a chair and Marie-Claude had her head in the microwave while Gus manned the controls. I heard Marie-Claude's voice: "Give me thirty." Then Gus's nervous glance caught my own. He nodded and I found myself nodding back.

This is my favourite brand of soap. You should know
this about me. This soap feels best on the skin. It's gentle
enough for my face, but also has the cleansing power to cut
through the worst dirt and grease. Car oil, tree sap, ink from
an exploded ballpoint, blood. Never dries the skin. This
is such wonderful soap. I keep a bar of it by the sink and
another in the shower and another in the kitchen. Smell it.
Go on. Light spicy odour, almost nothing. Inhale. Tingles
the nose. And feel the creamy texture, the soft exfoliant.
Poppy seeds for a natural, massaging scrub. Now try it on
your hand. Right against the skin. Rub it in little circles.
Like this. Round and round. See how it buffs the skin on
your forearm? See how it brushes away those dry patches
on your shoulders? Let's try some water. This is simply
one of my favourite products. Check the lather. Heals,
soothes, moisturizes, in fact nourishes the hair and scalp
as it washes. Round and round. Soothing around the neck,
no? Over your shoulders. Round and round, round and
round. Is your forehead tingling yet? And behind the ears.
Those filthy, hard to reach places. Let me show you. Come
on. You could do dishes with this brand of soap. Amazing.
Bacon fat and burnt cheese. French fries. All around your
nostrils. Grease and more grease, the deepdown grime,
sweat glands. Those lips. Shouldn't be the least bit sour.
Don't worry. Hardly any sticky residue to speak of. A bit
like toothpaste, yes a bit like toothpaste, but more frothy,
creamy, more cleaning power, really gets between the
teeth, penetrates the enamel. Stains. See? Tough on those
disgusting germs, mouth, good for the teeth, good for the
tongue. The poppy seeds could be said to gratify the gums,

indulge the lingual membranes and saliva glands; it could be said to satisfy, luxuriate and even complete the mouth. No plaque here. Open up. You should really just relax, this is one of the finest products on the market. Wider. It's really dirty in there and without this soap we'll never be able to get you clean.

Within the rotating cast of ill-suited roommates, something clicks. They undressed in front of each other and fell asleep in each other's beds without the slightest awkwardness or pressure. The weather steadied itself and they soon realized that they could fall from here to there, from the chair or counter, safely to their own feet. They realized instinctively how to fit into the space reserved for them and became comfortable. The roof had been repaired and the walls had been painted. Their parents came to visit and were proud of their children's decisions. They stopped thinking about themselves, and engaged in some idle chitchat. They shared snacks. Some of their favourite words were "inkling," "profusion" and "overwhelm." Drinks were served and, at times, they noticed their conversation would turn to the salacious. They learned new ways to entertain themselves. They stopped talking long enough to hear their breathing. It was a nice day to marry, they thought, following the advice of the economy. In the afterglow, the days grew as long as their hair.

He looked about as happy to see me as I was to see him. The dinner had been delirious with Jane buzzing around her place, attending to the pots on the stove, and setting out the plates and food. Organic Chardonnay? She had swapped her usual cargo pants and pull-over for jeans and a shirt that went off her shoulders. Her books and stacks of papers had disappeared; everything was abnormally tidy. She stopped a few times throughout the meal to sit on my lap. The doorbell came as a complete shock, as did the sight of Dustin stepping into the apartment with his own goddamn bottle of Chardonnay.

He recovered more quickly than I, and was quickly into the jokes and witticisms, making, it seemed to me, a concerted effort to include me in his merriment. In the living room I sulked for about a minute, looking over at Jane with a look meant to simultaneously convey "I'm fine" and "What the fuck is he doing here?" I quickly realized that I'd better straighten up, get hold of the situation. When he said he had finished the Ovalle novel, I was able to come up with questions that made it clear he hadn't finished it at all. When he told another joke, I actually listened and went red with laughing. Jane poured some more wine as Dustin seemed to withdraw in his chair.

At some point the words gained sharpness. Dustin seemed to be on the defensive while I felt trapped in a cycle of wishing I'd been the one to show up in the Ogari shirt... mine is clearly better...while of course being glad I didn't. My stomach muscles fatigued as I tried to hold my stature tight, keep my movements strong and smooth. He in turn strained to maintain a semblance of joviality. We were sweating. For awhile we didn't even seem to acknowledge that Jane was there at all. She hugged me from the back and Dustin's face was now undeniably pained. "Why are you doing this?" he asked her. I could feel my balance go shaky. Jane's voice was calm: "No scene, okay?" She pulled him over to us and immediately found a place in between. Taking the lead, I lifted her shirt over her head, unclasped her bra and from somewhere found the nerve to grab Dustin's head and pull his face between her tits. Jane mumbled incoherent approval and pushed back against me. On the bed, Jane lay on her back, and I knelt leaning against the headboard and guided my penis into her mouth. Another sip of wine did nothing to prevent the nearly incapacitating pulse of my temples. The outline of Dustin's head was visible as it moved between Jane's legs and she was going crazy. When she flipped around and the condom was finally on, I pushed my cock into her. Dustin kneeled in front of her for a while, leaning back on his hands, then cursed and stepped off the bed. It was dark but I could see the silhouette of his head as he came up to me and looked into my face. Against mine, his lips were tight and tentative. He swore again and I heard him flop into the armchair in the corner of the room. Jane's fingers were on the backs of my thighs as she rocked back onto me. I watched his shadow over there in the corner until it, and everything else, went dark.

To be spell bound is the only goal in this apartment, the world's ceiling. When one is widowed and late in life moves to the city to begin again or perhaps see things through to the end, it's prudent to delight in some of the oldest tricks: the small blue flowers, the precise engineering of the watch, the warm vibration of the cat purring, the tangible shape of electricity when the radio signal goes fuzzy. This is ecstasy, she thinks, the gleam of things in those overlooked places where the gaze has forgotten to pause. The shapes that weigh nothing. Here, where structure becomes sky, they float upwards in a low banter: "Emptiness?" "A lark!" "Static? Finished?" "Both of them, over and done with!" They literally raise the roof. And inside the space, the continual pleasure of the most apparent oversights revealing themselves: door, window, scar, system. Instead of the strident dead end of walls, a clandestine tunnel to the source of the festivity, which is as open and sudden as a first or last breath.

First the television begins to recede, then the bantering voices of the news anchor and the sports-reporter. "You mean it's NOT good to stretch before exercise?" asks the anchor in an exasperated tone. On the chesterfield the teen-ager nestles his head into the warm lap of his first girlfriend. His T-shirt is riding up his back and she draws pictures on his spine with her fingernail. A house, a dog, a man playing piano, Liberace, stretched triumphant across the keyboard having a hard time containing his teeth gums tightening red pull white face stiff going eyes as he realizes he's under-water… the man in the parking garage has the appearance of a convicted felon, a car thief perhaps, leather jacket and ball cap, tinted glasses and pockmarked skin. "Why do girls like to be fingered with this one best?" he asks, stroking the knuckle of his middle finger. "Because it's mine." He'd be even creepier if you didn't already know that he was a perverse prophet, sent here to this parking garage to deliver two important pieces of advice: "It's not very important what you do. What is way more important is the state of mind from which you are doing it," he says, and, "Careful not to lose your wallet." He hands you his business card and runs… in the pool the naked girls, slippery as seals, one by one releasing their breath between the blue lips of the Man from Glad who's panicking, coughing underwater before he realizes he can breathe, laughing, voice hoarse as he notices a crustacean scurry on the bottom of the pool up his leg into his pants, sweating sprawled there dozing the teenager notices the rough upholstery of the chesterfield against his skin, the indoor afternoon heat, feels his girlfriend's hand on his neck, crawling itsy-bitsy up the spout.

3442 rue St. Dominique

Her life in fortune cookies and newspaper clippings.

Good things will come your way. Your baby teeth will drop out painlessly. Doors will swing open for your entry. You will consume a thousand pounds of sugar. Patience is your strongest attribute. You will begin to suit your clothes. Your loyalty will be rewarded. The length of your legs will soon be in style. A pleasant surprise waits in store. Your house will survive the earthquake. You will bruise your arm in a boating accident. You will walk the padded road. Pride in your work will yield great rewards. An emotional breakdown will teach you more than you know. The mole on your stomach is malignant and will have to be removed immediately. You will be lucky with love. Your parents will die before you. The skin under your chin is starting to droop. Someone will heed your bad advice. People want to be you, you want to be someone else. Your children will die after you. The joys of leisure will be yours. You will become lazy in your old age. Your eyes will slowly cloud over. Almost there. You will fall from an airplane that is about to crash and land on a patch of soft grass.

… there's something in the water. Hard to keep things straight. Here it's all microbiology. Olivia, next door, keeps going in for operations. Everyone I meet has a year-round suntan. Then there are the doctors: their matching SUVs, their hysterical laughter. The building itself seems alive, or like a virus living through us, those who live here. Thus the architecture of my chest cavity, my hearthearthearthearth… hear the art, earth, hear it…. I push my fingers into the hole behind the bathtub slowly, with fear and anticipation, then bring them to my nose. Sticky dampness. Two days ago I discovered an old plumbing pipe out back that dispenses toasty knitted winter slippers. I put a pair on and they fit perfectly, as if they were designed specifically for me.

Buckskin headspin. The narcotic throb of collapsing into a firm chair in the early evening, drooping onto a table in a small, unfamiliar kitchen. It's been three cups of tea and the visitor feels his bladder swelling. Neither nicotine nor caffeine have taken hold. Across the table the resident slumps her head into her palm for support. He's here to borrow a hair dryer. Close by there's the sound of a loud crash followed by a long groan, a dinnerware accident downstairs. The two of them sip their tea. There's something monastic about these rooms—an ambience of seclusion, method and ritual—that makes this space seem cell-like, more like adobe Pueblo housing than a city row house. The air ripples. Most city apartments are usually designed in terms of human anatomy but this apartment seems more like a series of self-repeating units—more like organ tissue or coral, more like a hive. It takes another cup of tea to pull himself off the tabletop and another cigarette to stand up. His head's so tired he can't look up. Jaw so heavy he's speechless. He's unable to say how good it feels.

… again you speak to me with careful words that show you have nothing more to say. Whenever I fear that I have become impervious to that heavy weight in the abdomen, that I've hardened myself beyond repair, it happens again. I know I should extract myself, minimize the damage, but I will stay to watch you depart from me every time. The idea of you is treacherous to the actual you. I will endure anything to keep you there, fixed in my mind, walking away with the promise to return. I would permit myself to bow to my own ignorance just to preserve this safety. I would leave all wounds unattended. I am not the satellite of anything. For you I would cease idolizing the soul. For you I would praise the absence of soul.

1037 rue Gertrude

The neighbourhood grocery store constituted the ground floor of the building. The magazine rack was moved upstairs after the store closed and the building was sold off suite by suite. For the boy, the store had been the heaven of all luxuries. He would pour himself slush drinks, take chocolate bars at will, and was allowed to use the motorized slicer to cut himself pieces of salami. Throughout the day he could be behind the counter and sometimes make change or help spoon the balls of ice cream into the cones. He could play in the walk-in cooler and was the envy of all the kids on the block. When he came in with a friend, his grandfather would give them chips or ice cream, so there was no shortage of children who wanted to spend time with him. His grandfather was a small, spindly man who kept the store open from dawn to dusk. His non-existent conversation skills and knobbed frame was a result of the war. He always seemed to be fading away. He'd hand out free snacks and allow the whole neighbourhood to run up bills they could never pay back. In the photograph he stands in front of the magazine rack, with a drab apron and a massive chocolate rabbit. His grandfather's eyes are vacant and, with the snow piled up outside the window, he's hard to make out. Each Easter he would give the rabbit away to the person who could accurately guess its weight. The magazine rack is filled with comics, crossword books and women's magazines, much as it is now. In the waiting room of the suite upstairs, the dentist's patients enjoy the abundant selection of reading material, his nice selection of treats. While waiting for the hygienist to take them in, they sometimes recognize the rack in the picture.

Generally the gentlest of creatures, the pet would occasionally turn belligerent when in heat or when someone interrupted its feeding. It would mark the apartment with a scent that was both warning and threat. And yet it always displayed a strong sense of pathos for its owners, and would show overt signs of guilt and grief after any such outburst.

Pacing the rooms, hot under the scalp, stewing in the bathroom, hall and pantry, ready to hurt shit. *I'm not at home. Please leave a message.* The air is sweat and you're swimming in it. You're losing your way, always rented rooms, painted wood floors, hallways and hallways, sloping walls and you're losing your sense of direction, always too humid or cold, stuck windows, double rooms, parties and landlord fuck. *Come near me and I'll make your throat. One step closer and you'll be touching cloth.* And it's sticky and you're fanning yourself, running fast, turning, spinning so fast in the bedroom, little table, little drawers, so hot, burn, calm, slow yourself and breathe, stop twisting, settle by the open window. Air, you need air, yes, and breeze, that's good, sit down and breathe.

Apt. d'Amours

The four movements of a scientific opera: postulation, method, data-collection and conclusion. Four chapters to a novel with an uncertain storyline. I found the notebook under some paper on her bookshelf. Casually hidden. The first thing I do when I'm alone in someone's home is locate his or her diary. So I'm sitting on the sofa. Even though the door is locked, and she's not due back for an hour, I keep looking over my shoulder as I read. Dr. Wendt thinks it's the guilt that turns me on. I think she might be right. With obvious disappointment she declared my confession to be a substantial setback in my progress and I didn't have the nerve to tell her about the keys I had already copied.

Until the orange juice hit the back of his throat, he had no idea how dry his throat actually was. *How can I love you in the shape I'm in?* He stood on the front balcony awhile to catch his breath, then walked through the many small rooms of the apartment to the back balcony. The architect of this building designed each room of the apartment to have its own narrative progression, like a story. Oddly, he placed all the narrative tension at both ends of the apartment, namely the balconies, rather than in the rooms themselves. This was the architect's last building before committing suicide. The inhabitant finds him- or herself drawn to these structures, but at the expense of the rest of the rooms, which are rendered lifeless and anticlimactic. Coming in off the balcony, the present occupant finds himself strangely bored and disappointed with the interior as if, like a mediocre novel, the momentum of the apartment has come to an abrupt halt. He pours some more orange juice. Within minutes, he is drawn back to the balconies, the view of Mount Royal, the city's sidewalkscape, staircases and front yards, passers-by and traffic. *Bearing the weight of laziness.* It's becoming a problem. The plants by the front window are wilted and dead. The dog dish is dry, and the puppy sways on its legs. The gun over the mantle remains untouched, never to appear in the story again.

The baby girl was a quick learner, having synthesized a full range of traits from both of her parents, the charming and the devious. Of all the toddlers in the neighbourhood, she was the first to learn to read and also the first to tear out the pages. Within months she mastered the grilling of the steaks and soon thereafter presented reasons to not grill the steaks. She was the first to promote a new visceral style of physical comedy as a means to reinvigorate the social potential of satire, and the first to declare the movement over. She appreciated the qualities of movement and speed, but also understood the necessity of slowness and leisure. She quickly learned the importance of ladders. She invented games with numerous chess boards, matches and glasses of unfinished wine.

Her parents, being both responsible and duplicitous people, came up with a plan to protect themselves, their apartment and belongings, while also providing an environment to encourage the open development of their daughter's obvious talents. They scheduled time off work, put on their pajamas and let the routines of the apartment go. They put their most cherished books right at her eye-level and gave her a chrome lighter. They blended the contents of the fridge and poured it into bowls they left on the floor. They took to napping in the living room, waking only to wipe their noses on the picture books and look blankly at the costumed characters on the TV shows. They made a fuss for their daughter's attention and cried when she wandered off; they bit or punched each other when she was out of the room, and accused the other when she came in, looking frustrated. They made a mess of their pants when she drank too much, and let her figure out the fire extinguisher when their cigarettes set the blankets smouldering. They made her laugh with cute songs and then put clothes pins on the cat's tail.

Eventually things found their rhythm. More than once the three of them found their faces waxened with tears, unable to decide if they had been crying, laughing, or if it had all been a reflex, like drooling. They took turns in the bath. Parents and children—it is odd when you trigger instinctive behaviour in either of them—like survival, like nurture. It's alright to test their capabilities, but they can hurt themselves if they go too far. It can be helpful to imagine them all gorging on their favourite food until their bellies ache. Fall came and the family went to school together.

"I can't believe I said that," he thinks, holding his arms against his chest to keep warm. "That was so stupid. She must hate me."

Up the stairs to the top floor and onto the metal ladder which leads to the roof. A flock of pigeons in a never-ending cluck, all standing on one leg with their beaks nestled in their feathers. A view of the university clock tower, the cemetery on the hill. The video monitors are located in a small attic space off the roof: a monitor for each suite. Where are the cameras hidden? Inside their apartments, the residents are engaged in what at first seems like everyday activities. The woman in the bachelor suite vacuuming, Jean's kids sprawled on the couch, the doctors talking at their kitchen table. What becomes noticeable though is the degree to which their movements seem studied, practiced. On a table by the monitors there is what appears to be a large black button inset into the wood of the table. Am I making it up? I run my hand over it. "Stop!" Jane is there, holding open the flap of the attic door and looking down. "You shouldn't be seeing this."

The gardenias shriveled into cacti. The CD player tripped on a circuit, sending the singer into an endless rendition of *Easy Living*. The cat pounced in its sleep. The mirror kicked up dust bunnies while the refrigerator turned over like an overheated car. Entering the room she switched on the television and upset the electrical field. The night cleared its throat for a second, then fell silent. She had been dreading this moment for so long that, once it finally happened, she was unsure as to what her original reservation might have been.

His mouth is just another wrinkle on his face.

"Sea birds don't feed their babies as often as land birds do. The babies may get fed once a day or even once every five or ten days. Land birds, such as robins, eat many times each day. In just one day a baby robin may eat ten feet of earthworms."

He's just a head. His beige sweater matches the fabric of his chair identically and it's impossible to make out where his neck begins.

"Most birds do not sing when it is raining very hard. This is also true when there is a strong wind. Birds don't sing much when it is very hot or cold. However, it has been noticed that birds sing more than usual just before or after a storm."

His words seem pre-inscribed in space ahead of him. His voice plods forward in a mechanical lull that allows you to slip into a meditative state of advanced thought-processes. In his presence you can sit for hours, entranced by your own thoughts, without having to actively engage in conversation.

"Don't water your plants when the sun is shining on them. It is better to water them at the beginning or end of the day. Water on the leaves of plants acts as a lens. The water makes heat from the sun even hotter and, as you know, too much heat burns the leaves."

Think of fingers, teachers, cars, the contents of your wallet.
Pleasure, revenge, sleep, people who would kill to be you.
Think of rice, rivers, Tropicalia, chicken, hallways, pipes,
paper, telephone banking, vine.

Apt. d'Amours

Jane's avoiding me, as are the others. I woke up last night hearing some voices—a small group—outside my door, but by the time I opened it the crowd had dispersed. I could hear their doors click shut in the hall. I had just gone back to bed when I heard a light knock at my door. It was Hélène, the legal secretary, with her kid. She gestured for me to lean in with her finger: be careful, she warned. And today, the animated voices behind doors in the Apt. d'Amours, people meeting, parties everywhere. Something is being planned, and it seems as if it involves me.

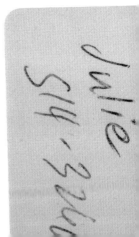

4808 rue de Grand Pré

The hot water prickles his scalp for a second, but it feels good. With his goggles on he can see the amount of particulate matter floating in the bath water. He draws some of the hot liquid between his lips, watches the bubbles ascend to the surface of the tub, then expels the water. He tries again. He sucks the water into his mouth, holds on to it for a moment, and then squirts it out underwater. FFFFFFTTT. Once more. Now with your lungs. He isn't sure what to expect. A burning, coughing sensation, a sharp tickle? Nothing. He opens his eyes. He finds that he is able to pass the water in and out of his lungs without any difficulty.

Glaring afternoon light. Pawn to Queen four. "No, wait." Bouvard and Pecuchet are playing chess in the livingroom. Couches and chairs, a room for sitting in. Stage left, a whistle suddenly breaks the silence. Neither of them look up. They massage their hands. They hesitate. One two three. Paper covers rock. Bouvard licks his fingers while Pecuchet pulls up his sleeve, exposing his forearm. "Wait." A whistle sounds, stage right. A glass of red wine descends slowly from the ceiling and settles on the coffee table. Whistle from above. Without looking up Bouvard and Pecuchet reach simultaneously for the wine. Their hands touch. You're it. They lean back in their couches, look at their thighs and hesitate. "Two out of three."

Apt. d'Amours

My face is an imitation of itself. What are you? I ask it.
What in God's name are you? "I'm Leukaemia. I'm blood
trouble."

The viewer enters a single large rectangular brick room. Once a second-floor warehouse space for the fabric store below, it is now the apartment of three enterprising room-mates. The activity, like something from Borges, takes place in front of the long, brick sidewall of the space. It costs five dollars. The inhabitant leads the viewer to a place about halfway down the wall, where the wall is buckling under its own weight. The bricks have become loose over time and lost their surface tension: the wall looks almost liquid. After staring at the wall for a number of minutes, the viewer notices a number of missing bricks in the structure, an almost percussive pattern of absences. Images appear. The physical effect created by these holes is at first one of perceptual discombobulation: the room opens up on itself, giving one the sense that the wall is more of a mirror than a dividing structure. The viewers of this apartment are amazed to find themselves on the other side of the wall, looking out into the loft, they become entranced with the psychological confusion and general denial that comes with confronting one's own double. *What sort of contraption...?* Sometimes one is so bewitched by the effect that a kind of addiction arises: many viewers return frequently to the apartment, desiring other glimpses of themselves. Other times, this amazement gives way to terror. The viewer suddenly realizes that he or she has been absorbed into a structure that is in fact one's own body. Dizziness and nausea have been known to ensue.

... laughing in the pipes, laughing from all sides. The neighbours are taunting me. I rip the plastic off my window, throw it open. The first buds are out on the trees and there's a faint hint of spring on the air. Will I make it? Putting out my garbage I opened the dumpster to find a large plastic biological waste barrel. I reached inside and pulled the lid to one side. Operating gloves, intravenous bags, even some mucous-like substance in thick plastic bags. Smell overpowering. When I turned around I noticed their faces staring at me from various windows. Mr. Green, Dustin, Mme. Lafrenière, the politician, Olivia, Jean the teacher, even Jane. Impassive expressions, looking at me without any real interest, but looking nonetheless. I lock the door, block it with furniture.

The whole apartment vibrates as the trucks go by outside, shakes when the train passes. Bricks creak. Drops of condensation roll down the walls. It's still dark when the two of them hear the sound of the kids downstairs splashing around in the inflatable pool. The window is open and the fan is making far too much noise for sleep. The air hangs under the weight of itself. On the desk there's a glass of warm juice and an almost-evaporated fish tank with an earwig twisting around in the water like some crazy bait. They're sweating too much to consider getting up, their breath coming too slow. It's almost morning. They hear the sprinklers come on in the park and listen to someone upstairs taking a shower. "What about the elderly?" one of them whispers, unable to laugh. They know it'll end like this. Bloated and itchy, drowning in the warm pool of themselves. In the distance an ambulance siren breaks the silence of the returning heat.

Apt. d'Amours

My bags are packed; they sit in lines at the door. All I have to do is pick up the phone and call a taxi, carry my bags to the corner and wait. But I can't. I know the *À Louer* sign on the door is for me, a less than subtle hint that I'm not welcome here, but that makes me want to stay to see it through. I put on my shoes and coat, and stand by the door. I catch myself waiting for something. I pick up my bags and put them down. The longer I stand the more I become certain that I will never leave the Apt. d'Amours, never tell a soul what I've seen.

Somewhere else in town, a man is waiting for his taxi to the airport. His keys are on the kitchen table. He takes a last look around the place to make sure he's not leaving any last items that he simply cannot do without, as well as any information that could help his landlord track him down later. Apart from some clothes, essential reading, and a few cherished knick knacks, hastily stuffed into the pockets of his bags, he's abandoning his furniture, posters, kitchen ware, portable stereo, albums and books as he abandons the apartment. Perhaps the items will be of some value to the landlord who, he realizes, probably doesn't deserve this, or the unpaid rent. The utilities have been shut off, without a forwarding address given. The back door has been locked to help minimize any break-ins before the landlord comes by to find the front door unlocked, the suite empty. Out of guilt, the man puts a $50 bill next to the keys: the landlord will likely have to hire someone to remove some of this stuff. He opens the door to the shower stall which is built off the hallway itself, and the door of the tiny closet that houses the toilet. No time to clean at this point; he puts another $20 on the table. He thinks of who might be there, waiting for him when he arrives. They are close, he thinks. They will find each other. His new life takes a step ahead of him, ahead of the death rattle of his old life, and he follows it through the door. Outside the cab has arrived and is honking insistently.

The infinite flickering of the bathroom light finally becomes noticeable. Somewhere there's a drought, you can feel it on your skin. Somewhere a river's drying up, the speed of light slowing to a trickle. For a moment the moths strobe in confusion before disappearing with the walls, sink, bulb, into a new definition of black: stolen black. Sounds brush your ears like an afterimage flash on the retina. Where's your head at? A moment ago you were looking at yourself in the mirror, thinking of returning to bed. There was soap and warm water. If you strained your ears, you could just make out the rustle of someone tossing around in the bed next door—filthy dreams perhaps, the kind that are hard to wake from. Now the inside of this room no longer exists and the whole idea of expiry dates is an unlikely thing to be thinking about in the dark, as are body-snatchers. "The spaces between," you hear her mumble through the walls. You can't inhale for the silence. Your breath is taken away.

Apt. d'Amours

You go missing inside yourself the odds are two to three you won't come back. The hunter knows the value of a fresh kill. He bends over your body and squeezes your neck. You're too far gone. Or when your skin ignores your body and it's the bone in your forearm that notices your scratching. There are distractions you stray into only in retrospect. The television is all static and you realize the cigarette cherry has been too close to your eyes.

Author's Note

To respect the privacy and wishes of a number of Montreal apartment dwellers, the first edition of this publication contained some necessary omissions. This new edition reinstates most of the original manuscript, with the exception of a small percentage of material that remains too personal, inflammatory or ill-wrought. By now, most of the people documented and dramatized herein have found new domiciles. Many have changed career paths, found new partners and friends, moved elsewhere. Some of us have grown apart even beyond the limitation of distance. Some of us never really knew each other at all. Time has allowed these new texts to emerge with some degree of safety and perhaps a shred of propriety. *Walkups* was never meant to be the work of a paparazzo.

With the exception of one of the apartments, which was gutted by fire, all can be seen more or less as they were. Rents are higher. The Apt. d'Amours are still there too, not far from the bike path in Rosemont, looking slightly tarnished. The significant and mundane dramas of these living spaces continue to unfold in narratives of interiority and domesticity. It is more than likely that some readers will know people who have inhabited these spaces, or at least know the apartments themselves. *Walkups* remains unfinished.

Lance Blomgren was born in Cumberland, British Columbia and currently lives in Dawson City, Yukon. His most recent book *Corner Pieces*, a collection of short fiction and urban proposals, was shortlisted for the Relit Award in 2005. His text, *Liner*, won the bpNichol Chapbook Award in 1998. His stories, essays and text-projects have been published and presented internationally.

From 1995 to 2005, Blomgren resided primarily in Montreal, Quebec. A radio version of *Walkups*, in collaboration with artist Samuel Roy-Bois, was produced by the CBC in 2003. A French-language edition of the book, translated by Élizabeth Robert, was released in 2007.

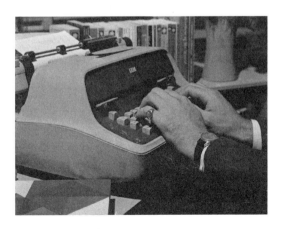